SNOOKERED

(Снукер)

Don Allen

ISBN: 979-8-9921997-9-6

eISBN: 979-8-9932322-0-1

Publisher: Don Allen

Also, by Don Allen

1 Dream

I was running through a field of snow, snow up to my knees. I was struggling. My destination, a small block house on the edge of the field. The faster I ran, the further away it became. Something terrible was about to happen, and only I could stop it. But I had to get to that block house first. I ran on, my legs feeling like weights were tied to my feet.

Then there was a blinding light. The snow around my legs disappeared. I was standing on scorched earth. Nothing alive, not even ants. I cried out – Maggi was shaking me.

"You were dreaming," she said. "You scared ltl' George."

2 A Quiet Morning

I was home, spending a quiet morning with my son, ltl' George, not so little now, he is almost ten, and Maggi, my significant other. She was still opposed to marriage, didn't want to give up the freedoms a single lady has in Greece. Home was the island of Corfu. Together, we ran Basdakis Shipping Brokerage Co.

As a condition of being together, she insisted I stop working with my Uncle Christos, an antique dealer in Biloxi, Mississippi. His main activity was smuggling Greek artifacts. I came to Greece to manage my uncle's operations from this end, well, that and the fact that at the time, I was on the FBI's wanted list in Miami.

My youthful indiscretions were behind me now, thanks to the statute of limitations. My assistance in closing a notorious South American drug ring that had the FBI flummoxed also helped.

My Uncle Alexander, a senior agent in the Greek Intelligence Service, recruited me into the GIS's web of intrigue as I transitioned from criminal indiscretions to more acceptable societal indiscretions. The GIS had a close working relationship with its British counterparts, MI5 and MI6. Basdakis Shipping provided a plausible cover for the clandestine operations that they concocted.

Recently, I was involved in a small task for MI6 aimed at disrupting the flow of weapons to insurgents in the Horn of Africa. The CIA conducted the operation, but the arms dealers were former British subjects. Perhaps this was the cause of my dream.

Although Maggi liked Uncle Alexander on a personal level, she refused to take his calls since they normally led to me being absent for several months.

Our landline was ringing. "Don't answer that damn thing," yelled Maggi.

I answered. It was Alexander. "Can you pop over to Athens in the morning?" he asked. "Our friends in the Misty Isles have a problem."

I arrived in Athens early the next morning, arriving on Ellinair flight 95. I was met at the airport by Kostas Doukas, one of Alexander's people. I first met Kostas in Singapore after a freighter found me adrift in the Indian Ocean. Another clandestine mission that went sideways.

Kostas' sole job at that time was to get me home. He did, but after a side trip to Zimbabwe to claim my interest in a small gold mine that Fat Leonard and had I bought into.

While there, MI6 enlisted me to investigate Chinese poaching of rare-earth minerals, lithium specifically.

Oh, the gold mine, it was productive until it wasn't; the new political regime confiscated the mine and most of the profits. I was lucky to get out of the country. Maggi was placated somewhat when I was able to produce a hundred thousand euros that I had earlier transferred to my Greek bank account.

"George, good of you to come on such short notice," said Constance Gabris, the Director of GIS. "Alexander was reluctant to call on you so soon after your last mission, but Sir Charles was insistent that you be called in." Sir Charles being the head honcho at MI6.

"The problem in the 'Misty Isles' is that weapons are being smuggled into a commonwealth Nation," said Constance. "Your recent adventure in Djibouti makes Sir Charles think you are the man for the job."

About then, Uncle Alexander came into the conference room. He was accompanied by Detective Inspector Harold Lynn. Harold worked for MI5 until he was placed on a long-term MI6 assignment. Harold was with me in Djibouti

3   Recruitment

Alexander picked up the narrative. "The Commonwealth Nation in question is Kenya. Kenya may face a full-blown insurgency on its coast unless President William Ruto can douse a combustible mix of ethnic rivalries, land rows, and Islamist militancy. Gunmen have killed about 500 people this year, exposing festering problems that could test Ruto's ability to reassure a nation fretting about wider security. He has asked for the Commonwealth's help."

"We know that weapons are being smuggled to these groups," said Harold. "We don't know the where, the how, or the who." Sir Charles has his suspicions that tie back to Isabel. That is why he has requested GIS to loan you to MI6.

"Well, I'm flattered that you all have such high faith in me, but I must decline. I promised Magie that I was done with the cloak 'n dagger stuff'.

"George, can I have a word with you in private?" said my Uncle.

As we stepped out into the hall, Alexander turned to me, "George, you are family, but I have to set that aside. We need you to do this. Isabell is your cousin and a distant member of the British Royal Family. She may or may not be involved, but we need to control the story."

"Harold is capable of doing that," I said. "I'm going home."

"No, George, you're not. Unlike the American judicial system, the Greek system has no statute of limitations. I've suppressed information documenting your plundering of Greek artifacts with my brother. I have an extensive folder hidden away. I'd like to keep it that way, but ..."

"You're blackmailing me?!!"

"Well, not to be so crude about it, but yes. We need you."

After a few more heated words, we stepped back into the conference room where Alexander announced, "George is on board."

"Okay, Harold, pack your bags, we're going to Kenya," I said.

"No, no, I'm just Sir Charles's messenger. I need to get back to London."

About then, Constance spoke up. "Harold, here is someone who wants to talk with you," she said as she handed him her cell phone.

Harold takes it, puts it to his ear, and starts "Harold here, what can ..." and he is cut off, as the voice took over. After a very short one-sided conversation, he hands the phone back to Constance. "What time do we leave?"

Alexander whispered to Constance, "Who was that?"

"Sir Charles, he's been listening in."

"Okay," I said. "Harold and I will leave day after tomorrow. I need to placate Maggi. There is one thing you can do for me, *Uncle*: contact the CIA and see if they know where Madam Woo is. She's the major Chinese arms dealer in the Indian Ocean."

4 Isabell or is it Amira

The MET, London's police force, had closed Isabell's case, labeling it an unsolved murder. Isabell turned out to be my cousin, second or third, I'm not sure, through a convoluted family history as well as a member of the royal family.

Her grandmother, the Vice-Countess of Hinsdale, was impregnated by a second lieutenant from the Cheshire Regiment in the early '50s. The mother gave birth to a son. She was demoted to a baroness for incurring the Queen's displeasure. The lieutenant was shipped off to Malaysia where he became an admirer of the Gurkan solders in Her Majesty's Service.

My connection was through my great-uncle, a Greek refugee named Servopoulos, and a childhood friend of Prince Philip. Yes, that Philip, Queen Elizabeth's consort.

The lieutenant, Servopoulos's son, through an exemplary military career with the 2nd Gurkha Rifles, was awarded the title of Lord Ashfield and the accompanying estate upon his retirement. Servopoulos was my mother's cousin, my second cousin.

Isabell is the granddaughter of Lord Ashfield and the disgraced Vice-Countess of Hinsdale's son. She was fathered by Mathew, the bastard son.

As a young man, Matthew led a wildlife, a member of the Mediterranean jet set. He married Nadine, the daughter of Amal Choucair, an alleged Beirut arms dealer.

Isabell followed in her father's footsteps. She led a colorful life, having affairs with Members of Parliament and frequenting London's more base establishments. Her body, or a body the MET thought was hers, was found in a London alley. MI5 brought me in to find her killer because of the work I did the previous year on Lord Ashfield's security detail.

Due to circumstances described elsewhere, Isabell was not dead. On one of his routine visits to London, Alexander and Sir Charles speculated over a snifter of twenty-year-old Scotch that Amira, Amal's new protégée, was the reincarnated Isabell. Scuttlebutt had it that she was a hard-nosed taskmaster.

5 Nairobi

We landed at Nairobi's Jomo Kenyatta Airport late in the afternoon. Sir Charles had made reservations for us at the Sarova Stanley Hotel in central Nairobi. I was surprised; it was a five-star hotel.

We had a meeting with the Cabinet Secretary of the Ministry of Interior, Onesimus Kipchumba Murkomen, at ten the next morning.

With nothing to do, I said, "Let's take a foot tour and see what this place looks like." We were clearly in the business district, just on the edge of a complex of government office buildings.

"This place is definitely an upgrade over Harare," I said. I was in Zimbabwe's capital three years earlier. That was where I met Madam Woo, which reminded me, Sir Charles had not gotten back to me as to her current location.

Two blocks to the north, we found the Jamia Mosque with its twin minarets and three silver domes. Further on was the Jeevanjee Gardens, one of the city's landmarks.

"Enough random wandering," said Harold, "I'm hungry."

"We can try one of the street vendors," I joked.

Looking at the brochure he had taken from the hotel, Harold said, "There is a western-style restaurant around here somewhere. CJ's."

Five more minutes of wandering, we found CJ's and a decent meal.

The next morning, I asked the concierge for directions to the Ministry of Interior. He suggested walking; it was only five minutes by foot. A taxi in traffic at this time of day would take fifteen.

It took us seven. Navigating the building's security, I noticed several nervous young men with automatic rifles, fingers on the triggers. Upon entering, I told the receptionist we had an appointment with Mr. Murkomen.

Looking at us with some disdain, she said, "You mean the Honorable Murkomen?"

My stomach told me this was not going well, "Yes, I replied."

Looking at some papers in front of her, she said, "He's not available. You are to meet with Dr. Raymond Omollo. He is the Principal Secretary in the Department for Internal Security. I'll call his office and get you an escort." And with that, she returned to her magazine.

"Great," mumbles Harold. "Sir Charles talks with the President of the country, and we get shuffled off to a second-tier bureaucrat."

We were ushered into a conference room on the third floor. Dr. Raymond Omollo was waiting for us along with two others.

"Mr. Murkomen, the Department's Minister, asked me to take this meeting for him since it falls within my bailiwick. You must be George Basdakis and Harold Lynn. I'm Raymond Omollo. This is Mr. Sialaal Leley, Chief Executive Officer of the National Police Service. Next to him is Ms. Bernice Lemedeket, head of our National Intelligence Service."

After introductions and the shaking of hands, we were all on a first-name basis.

"I believe your mission here," said Raymond, "is to help identify the source of weapons being smuggled into Kenya. It hasn't been this bad since the 07–08 crisis. That was the crisis resulted in violent protests nationwide and an economic emergency. There were an estimated 1,500 deaths and 600,000 people displaced at that time."

Continuing, he said, "Porous borders with Somalia, Ethiopia, Uganda, and South Sudan facilitate the flow of illicit weapons, empowering both tribal militias and extremist groups to recruit and carry out attacks on the government and on each other."

"Our intelligence points to the Mombasa Republican Council as one of the main recipients of these arms," said Bernice. "The MRC is a radical group that believes Mombasa should secede from Kenya to become an independent state.

"The East Coast is experiencing the bulk of the violence," said Sialaal. "We don't have enough police assets to adequately patrol the area."

6 Mombasa

Harold and I thought it best to start in Mombasa. Our cover was the Basdakis Shipping Brokerage Co. My story, I was looking for new trading opportunities in East Africa. Harold was my bodyguard. The fact that he was a head taller than me and the MET's star rugby player helped the story.

We had reservations at the Hotel Sapphire, a three-star affair, in the city's business district that Raymond made for us. It wasn't bad, I've stayed at worse places.

I had the city map spread out on the bed, 'Where to start,' I was muttering to myself. Harold pointed to the Mombasa County Governor's Office. "It's near the Mombasa Golf Club, home of the Barry Cup," he said.

"What the hell is the Barry Cup?"

"The Barry Cup is the oldest golf tournament on the East Coast of Africa. With some luck, we might be able to find a soused official we can pump for information."

"That's not a bad idea," I said. "How do we get into the clubhouse? I'm sure it's members only."

14

"Well, I came up with the idea," he responded. "It's up to you to implement it."

Looking at Harold, I picked up the phone and asked the operator to connect me with the Chamber of Commerce.

A female voice came on the line, "Mombasa Chamber of Commerce, how can I help you?"

"This is George Basdakis. I'm the President of Basdakis Shipping. I'm in town looking for new business opportunities. I often find it convenient to visit an exclusive local club to meet its members and prospective clients. I was wondering if you could get me access to the Mombasa Golf Club this evening."

"Can you hold the line for a moment, let me catch Mr. Shikanda before he leaves. He's the club's vice president."

A moment later, "He said he'd be happy to have you as his guest tonight," she responded after coming back on the line.

"Thank you," I said, looking at Harold, "I will be bringing my assistant along."

7 Mombasa Golf Club

We arrived at the clubhouse just after seven. The parking lot was full. I was wearing a white linen sports jacket with a polo shirt. Harold was in a garish plaid sports coat, which did a poor job of concealing his shoulder holster. Our outfits were purchased that afternoon. We wanted to make an impression.

We were stopped by the doorman, about the same size as Harold, who politely informed us, "The club has a dress code," he said with a smirk, "and you obviously don't meet it."

"If you'd be so kind as to step aside, we are Mr. Shikanda's guests," I said with some bluster.

We were at a standoff until I heard someone calling my name. "Mr. Basdakis, I've been looking forward to meeting you," a pudgy middle-aged man of Indian descent said while guiding me into the lounge. The doorman stood there with a scowl on his face as Harold winked, followed us in.

"Mr. Basdakis, George, can I call you George? I'm Sunil Shikanda. Please call me Sunil. I'm the vice president of the

16

Mombasa Golf Club. I believe my secretary told you that. I'm also the Commissioner for trade development in Mombasa County. After your call, I had Mika, the young lady you talked with, do a quick search for Basdakis Shipping. I see that you have a well-established business in Greece, on Corfu, I believe she told me ..." and he rattled on for the next five minutes. Finally, "Mika indicated you wish to do business in Mombasa, is that right?".

"Yes, I'm looking for a small foothold in East Africa. I currently have a relationship with Varun Shipping in Mumbai. I am looking for a similar partner in this part of the world."

Harold almost choked on his beer. My relationship with the Varun Shipping Company grew out of a gemstone smuggling enterprise I established years earlier when I was in Zimbabwe. Since then, Rajee, the owner of Varun Shipping, and I have had a mostly above-board business relationship.

"Excellent, excellent," said Sunil. Mombasa has several shipping companies. We also have easy access to the interior of Africa."

"Yes, I know all that, but one concern I have is the recent civil unrest I have heard of. Your President, President William Ruto, has expressed concern about ethnic rivalries and Islamist militancy. Is civil unrest a real threat in the city?"

17

"No, no, not at all. There is Police Chief Simon Kigondu standing by the bar. Let me introduce you, and he can answer your question."

Looking toward the bar, I saw a man as black as coal and taller than most NBA players.

8 Simon Kigondu

"Simon, this is George Basdakis. He is considering opening a new outlet for Basdakis Shipping here in Mombasa. He is concerned about rumors of civil unrest in our community. I've told him they are baseless rumors. Maybe, as the chief of police, you can expand on my assessment."

Simon looked at me and then at Sunil, took a sip of his drink, and then said, "Civil unrest hell, we are on the verge of a second Mau Mau uprising!"

As Sunil turned three shades whiter, which was difficult due to his heritage, his chin bobbing, trying to find words, Simon broke into a loud, guffawing laugh. "You should see your face Sunil," he said, trying to catch his breath.

"George, please excuse me, I can never resist pulling Sunil's chain. This was just too good. As for civil unrest, no more so than the rest of East Africa. Some ethnic violence, yes, some gun running, yes. And unfortunately, a recent uptick in Islamic agitation."

"As you can see, Kenya is composed of diverse peoples. Sunil's people are from India. He's probably third generation. I'm Bantu."

"We also have a growing Arab and Persian population. As our Cultural Minister puts it, 'Kenya's ethnic diversity is not just a demographic reality but a cornerstone of our national identity, representing centuries of migration, interaction, and cultural exchange across the East African region.'"

"With that said," Simon continued, "the Arab community has brought with it some Islamic radicals. We have an active campaign to keep them under control." Simon said this with a wink, leading me to think that this control may be aggressively physical.

"And there are ethnic tensions. The Somalis have, for some time, been migrating south along the coast. The locals see them as infringing upon their land and fishing rights. There has been some armed resistance. Perhaps that is the source of the civil unrest rumors you have heard."

"This is all very interesting," I said. "It sounds as if you have it all under control, ... no impediments to expanding Basdakis Shipping to Mombasa."

Sunil was in full agreement, "Yes, everything is under control he echoed."

Later, as Harold and I left, Harold commented, "Under control hell. It's a powder keg with a lit fuse. I was talking with the bartender. DEI bullshit is taking hold here. As foreigners make up a growing part of the population, politicians play to them. Her brother-in-law just lost his fishing rights to the Somalis. He's considering joining one of the homegrown militias."

"Interesting. Where do they get their weapons? Maybe this is the lead we need," I said.

9 A Lead

"Harold, turn your charms on and call your new bartender friend, invite her over for coffee. If you call now, you should be able to catch her before the club closes."

After a comment not to be mentioned here, Harold pulls out his cell phone, "What's the number for the club?" I had jotted it down earlier in the day and had it with the business cards I collected that night. I handed him the card.

"Hello, earlier this evening I was talking with one of the bartenders, I think her name was Asya. Is she still there ... can I speak with her? Thank you."

Harold nods his head yes as he waits. "Asya. This is Harold. I was talking with you earlier tonight. I'd like to continue our conversation. Can we meet tomorrow for coffee before your shift? ... Yes, I'll find it. See you at five."

"She'll meet us at Jimmy's Tea Shop at five tomorrow. The tea shop is just outside the main entrance to the golf course."

Harold and I spent most of the next day wandering around Mombasa's port facilities, making a pretense that I was really looking to expand Basdakis Shipping.

I did find one small warehouse on the docks that was available. Under other circumstances, this would work quite nicely, I thought to myself. I could almost see myself calling Maggi, *'Darling, I just leased a small warehouse in Mombasa. You always said you wanted to expand our business.'* I could hear the blowback, even though it was just a thought.

We arrived at Jimmy's just before five. Asya was already there. She was a tall girl with a light brown skin tone.

"Asya, thank you for meeting us."

She was giving me the once-over. It was obvious my presence was a surprise.

"Asya, this is George Basdakis …"

And before he could go any further, she said, "No ménage à trois!" she snapped as she started to get up.

"No, no,' I protested, "you misunderstand. Harold was telling me about your brother-in-law's problems, and I wanted more information. I'm a journalist, you see, and I'm doing a story about cultural shifts in Africa."

Somewhat placated, Asya settled back into her chair.

"Harold told me your brother-in-law lost his fishing rights. His license was given to Somali immigrants under the country's new equity program. How did this happen?"

"The new County Commissioner, Stephen Kibunja, is a Kikuyu, one of the many Bantu tribes. Most of us on the coast are from the Mijikenda tribe, also Bantu. Kibunja was appointed by Nairobi politicians, many of whom receive bribes from the Somalis," she said.

"Harold said your brother-in-law is going to join a militia group."

"Yes, he already has."

"Are they armed, and who is the leader?"

"You are asking too many questions that can get me in trouble."

"Okay, I'm sorry. Can you introduce me to your brother-in-law? We might be able to help him," I lied.

Asya thought for a minute and then wrote down an address. "Meet me here tomorrow morning at ten. If I'm there, he will have agreed to talk with you."

10 Jacob Oyugi

The address Asya gave us was the Jahazi Coffee House on Ndia Kuu Road. It was not far from the Fort Jesus Museum, an old Portuguese coastal fort. This was an affluent section of Mombasa.

When we arrived, Asya was sitting at a sidewalk table. She pointed to two chairs. "Jacob will talk with you if you promise not to use his name in your article. He's afraid there will be reprisals against him if he is named."

"No names," I said. This was not a lie since there would be no article.

We ordered coffee and sat staring at the surroundings. "Where is your brother-in-law?" I finally said.

She waved her hand, and a middle-aged man who was sitting at a nearby table, appearing to be engrossed in the morning paper, moved his chair over to our table. "I'm Jacob Oyugi."

We introduced ourselves. I claimed I was a reporter for an English newspaper, and Harold was my bodyguard. I was starting a series of articles about the status of the Commonwealth nations. Kenya was my first. Jacob looked skeptical, so I showed him my press pass, which I had created for a moment like this.

Finally, "Okay, what do you want to know?"

I started with the information Asya had previously provided, and we went from there.

"You lost your fishing permit. What are you going to do?

"No, I lost permits for fifteen fishing boats. The fishermen in Magutu, a small village an hour north of here, no longer have jobs. The f... Somalis have taken them."

"Can't you fight this in court?"

Jacob laughed, "Our County Commissioner, Stephen Kibunja, controls the courts."

"I understand you have joined a local militia, is that right?"

"Yes, me and nine of my most trusted men!"

We ordered more coffee and talked for the next hour. Finally, I asked if he could take us to the next militia meeting. This took him by surprise. "Let me make a phone call," he said, getting up from the table and pulling his cell out when he was out on the street, out of earshot.

After a few minutes of Jacob walking back and forth, he returned to the table. "The Captain says you can come on two conditions. First, you will meet me here, and we go in a van with blackened windows, and second, you agree he can review what you write."

Three days later, Harold and I were back at the Jahazi Coffee House at eight in the evening. Jacob and Asya are waiting for us. Jacob is nervous as he asks for our phone. He takes them and hands them to Asya. "You get them back when we return."

There is an old VW van sitting at the curb. The windows had been painted. There is an interior cardboard screen between the back and front. Harold and I got in the back, Jacob driving, and Asya stayed at the coffee house. For an hour and a half, we bounced over every pothole in the city. The van had no springs. The last fifteen minutes felt as if we were on a dirt road. We finally came to a stop. The sliding door opened. We are beside a beach. A small coastal freighter was moored dockside close to a warehouse. Several other vehicles are parked along the road we just came down. The dust was still settling.

11 Kidnapped

"Okay, here we are,' said Jacob. "The Captain wants to meet you."

We entered through a side door; the space was dark. I could sense bodies around me, but they were unseen. Suddenly, the lights were on, and a spotlight was directed at Harold and me, blinding us. As my eyes adjusted, I saw Simon Kigondu ten feet in front of me, sitting on a packing crate. Next to him was Asya.

"George Basdakis, valued member of the Greek Intelligence Service, currently on loan to MI6. And Detective Inspector Harold Lynn," said Simon. "Let me give you a proper welcome to Kenya, a welcome worthy of spies. Your cover was good; I almost believed it until Asya told me of your interest in Jacob. Online research and a call to an old school chum in London told a different story. Now, why are you here?"

When I didn't answer, someone hit me behind my knees, and I dropped to a kneeling position.

"It's only going to get harder, George, if you're reluctant to talk. I know you are here to find the source of arms shipments to rebels in Kenya. Arms like these British assault rifles in this packing crate," he said as he patted the box he was sitting on.

"Oh, I know," said the Police Chief, "that President Ruto is worried about militia groups like this forming, but the old fool is allowing corrupt officials like Stephen Kibunja to give away our country just to placate international do-gooders. Now tell me, why are you here?"

"It sounds like you already know. If you keep talking, I will know ..." and the world went dark.

Later, I found Harold at my side, or more accurately, tied at my side.

"What happened? Where are we?" I asked through dry lips.

"The Chief was not amused by your answer. His man clubbed you. You've been out cold for over ten hours. I was getting worried. We're tied up in the cabin of the freighter we saw. We've been at sea for five or six hours," which would explain the hum of an engine that was racking my head, "so as to where we are, the best I can say is somewhere off the coast of East Africa."

As this settled in, Harold went on to tell me how Asya and Jacob had set us up.

"Asya was quite proud of deceiving a white man for the cause."

After a long period of silence, an older man in greasy coveralls came through the hatchway and took a seat on the other side of the cabin.

"Don't wanna-be too close," he said in broken English. "They tell me you dangerous. I captain of boat, Victor Shevchenko. They pay me to dump you at sea. Far away from beach. But maybe we do it now so you not worry. I have big men to help you over side."

About then, there was a shout from the bridge. Victor scrambled through the hatchway. A moment later, the engine was pushed to its maximum. We could feel the bow of the boat slapping against the waves. There were several bursts of automatic gunfire, some shouting, and the engine went dead. All this in under ten minutes.

Two men peered into the cabin, weapons at the ready. Seeing us, they gave a sigh of relief and entered the cabin. They addressed us in Urdu. I didn't speak Urdu, but I recognized it from an earlier excursion into Pakistan.

One pulled out a large, wicked-looking knife and sliced the rope binding us. They then motioned us to follow.

There were two bodies on the deck. Victor and two other men were sitting on the deck, held at gunpoint. Our rescuers cut some rope from a lifeline and tied the three to the bulkhead. There were two speedboats tied to the side of the craft we were on.

Our liberators pointed to a bench next to the three captives, indicating we should make ourselves comfortable as they restarted the engine and headed the small flotilla south.

12 Zanzibar

I didn't know it, but we were headed to Zanzibar, an island off the coast of Tanzania. Just as the engine was sputtering on the last of the fuel fumes, we entered a small port on the north end of the island.

At the dock, one of the men indicated that Harold and I should follow him. He had an old Land Rover. A five-minute ride along the beach brought us to a small touristy complex, the Flame Tree Cottages. Going through the lobby and out to the pool area, there was a collection of cottages. We were led to one in the back, off the beaten path, so to speak. He knocks, and a female voice says, "Enter."

Stepping into the room, I'm speechless. Sitting there with a cup of tea was Woo Lynn, better known as Madam Woo. The last time I saw Lynn was in Djibouti. Her parting words were, "Let's hope we don't meet again."

"Are you still smuggling arms to rebel groups for the Chinese?" I asked.

"And not so much as a thank you for saving you – again," said Lynn.

"Well, thank you. How did you know I was there?"

"I have ears in my competitor's camp. Victor has worked for me for several years. After you speak with Victor, which I know you want to do, I have to arrange for his escape."

"So, back to my first question, "Are you still smuggling arms to rebel groups? American weapons from Afghanistan?"

"Yes, and yes," was the response. "Victor works for my competition. I think you will find his information interesting."

***

Lynn was right. Victor was one of Amal Choucair's boat captains. He used to run contraband in the Mediterranean until Choucair, or was it his successor, expanded the operation into the Indian Ocean.

As he explained it, Amal had stepped back from the company. A young woman with 'brass balls' was running the operation.

"She mean bitch, some men don't like. She get results, pay good. Men cross her don't come back."

"Is her name Anira?" I ask.

"How you know that?"

Ignoring his question, I go on, "Where do you get your weapons from?"

"I go Odessa. Anira has contact. He load boat. Don't see weapons."

"Where do you deliver them?"

"Where Anira tell me! Small town Kenya, sometime other places. She give me coordinates and day, I go there."

13 Organized Escape

Later, "Victor's reliable," said Lynn. "I need to arrange a convincing escape, don't want his two crew members any the wiser."

"Where are they being held?"

"Tied in a shed down by the docks," she answered.

"Here is an idea. Have the guards talk, in a loud enough whisper so the two can hear about refueling Victor's boat. You plan to use it later in the week to move them to the mainland, where they will be sold. When Victor is escorted back to the shed tomorrow evening, after what appears to be an aggressive interrogation, he's thrown into the shed unconscious. I hope he's a good actor. That night, he has a miraculous recovery. The three overpower the guard and escape on the fully fueled boat.

"That might work," said Lynn.

The next day, Victor was brought back. Sitting over coffee, Madam Woo explained my plan. "Can you do that?" she asked.

"Yes, give me good bruis and cut on head. Need blood."

Also, I added, "Don't be surprised if you see me in Beirut, maybe even at Choucair's compound."

He looks at me but says nothing.

"Okay, good luck Victor," I said.

That evening, an 'unconscious' Victor was returned to the shack. At two the following morning, there was a quiet disturbance, and three shadows could be seen scurrying for the boat tied to the end of the dock. By quarter after, it had cast off and was pushing into the bay under minimal power, making little noise. It wasn't until after seven that the boat was reported missing.

14 Moving On

My cell phone was back in Kenya, probably repurposed by now. So, I had one of Lynn's men take Harold and me to a local phone store to buy new phones.

This was a problem in itself since I had no money. Harold told me my wallet and passport had been taken by Simon before I was dumped onto Victor's boat. They didn't want any identifying papers on our bodies in the event we washed up on the shore. I had to borrow money from Lynn.

The trip to the store was an experience in itself, but in the end, I was able to buy a relatively new Android phone. Harold deferred. The store owner promised it would work wonderfully, as long as I didn't stray too far from the cell tower on the northern end of the Island. He claimed he couldn't sell plans that provided service island-wide.

Back at the Flame Tree Cottages, Harold and I now had our own cottage. I called Sir Charles and reported our findings. I also asked him to cable money, a few thousand pounds, to the People's Bank of Zanzibar.

"You're planning on buying the place?" quipped Sir Charles.

"No, Harold and I could do with some new clothes. We really aren't dressed to fly first class on the flight you're booking for us. But joking aside, we need to get to Beirut to follow up on the weapons flowing into Kenya."

"This wouldn't involve an old friend, would it?" he asked.

"Yes."

And while we are talking about travel, Harold and I need new passports; ours were taken.

"I'll have two passports delivered to the bank. You don't mind being a British Citizen, do you, George?"

As we finished our conversation, he recommended that I return to Nairobi before going to Beirut to debrief Dr. Omollo.

That evening, I told Madam Woo that Harold and I would be leaving in the next few days -- if it was okay with her. After all, we were her guests, brought there under armed guard.

"Lynn, I know it's pointless to ask, but could you refrain from dealing with rebel groups in Kenya? I sort of told my masters that Harold and I had found the arms dealers, and they will be calling for increased international vigilance in East Africa. I don't want to see you getting caught up in it."

"George, I save your ass, again, and you turn on me, and then claim I'm your friend?"

As Lynn watched my conflicted face, she broke out laughing. "You should see your face," she said.

"To set your mind at ease, my masters in Beijing want me to close up shop and work with our diplomat weenies in Africa to earn the trust of Africans … and get access to the continent's natural resources like we did in Zambia."

15 Justice

I called Dr. Omollo as Sir George suggested. He was relieved to
hear from me. It had been reported that Harold and I were
kidnapped by arms smugglers and were probably shark bait by
now. He suggested we get back to Nairobi as quietly as possible.
He would make reservations for us, under false names, at the
'hotel' occasionally used by Ms. Lemedeket, head of the National
Intelligence Service

With a bribe or two, Madam Woo booked us on a flight under
false names from Zanzibar's Abeid Amani Karume airport to
Nairobi. Once there, I gave the taxi driver the address Dr.
Omollo provided. By nine that evening, Harold and I were
ensconced in downtown Nairobi.

Breakfast service in our suite was excellent. The hotel staff
obviously had prior practice.

At nine, Dr. Omollo called. "George, can you be ready by
nine thirty? I'll have my people pick you and Harold up."

His two men arrived on time and escorted us to the hotel's
loading dock where a limo with darkened windows was waiting.

We only traveled three blocks to the backside of the main court building. Using the service elevator, we arrived on the third floor, where we were quickly ushered into a closed conference room.

"Welcome," said Dr. Omollo, who was standing beside a coffee buffet. "Sorry for the secrecy. I wanted to make sure no one knew you were here; it would spoil the show later this morning. I'm going to leave you here for an hour or two. A guard will get you when we are ready. In the meantime, have some coffee and pastries."

Harold looked at me, his eyes saying, 'He'd had enough coffee to float a boat.'

We settled down and waited. Eventually, a security guard opened the door and motioned for us to follow. We entered the side door of a courtroom. Simon Kigondu, Mombasa's chief of police, was being questioned by Sialaal Leley of the National Police Service.

"Can you tell me again what happened to the two Europeans that you reported abducted?"

"Again?" he huffed. "As I've already testified, we were waiting for them at a community meeting. There was scuffling in the parking lot. By the time I got there, the ship had left the dock, and the driver, Jacob Oyugi, reported three armed men had just kidnapped his passengers, George Basdakis and Harold Lynn.

41

"You say this was a community meeting. What was the purpose of the meeting?"

"To find ways for the Mijikenda tribe and the new Somali immigrants to work together," Simon said with a somber face.

Dr. Omollo was sitting at the front of the room. He caught my eye and, without a word, motioned us to come forward. Simon Kigondu glanced over his shoulder and did the best double-take I have ever seen.

"Would you care to revise any of your testimony?" the Judge asked.

"If your Honor will indulge me," said Sialaal Leley I would like to play a short video my people made this morning."

"Okay, but keep it short," said the Judge.

"We executed a search of Asya Uhuru's home this morning. The video documents this search. As you can see, we are going through a drawer in her kitchen where we found passports for George Basdakis and Harold Lynn. Also found were two cell phones we believe belong to Basdakis and Lynn."

"Your Honor, if you would permit, I would like Mr. Basdakis to take the stand."

He permitted, and I testified, describing the events of the past few days.

"Where is this Madam Woo?" the Judge asked.

42

"That's what a lot of people want to know: she's elusive, preferring to remain in the shadows."

The Judge waved his hand, "Doesn't matter, I was just curious to meet her. Bailiff, take Mr. Kigondu into custody."

The two young security guards, the same two nervous guards with automatic weapons I had seen on my first visit, stepped forward and escorted Simon from the room.

16 Follow Up

As the courtroom cleared, Dr. Omollo came up beside me. "If you have a moment, my boss would like to meet with you."

Given that this was his country, his courthouse, and his armed guards, I said with a smile, "Of course."

We took the elevator to the sixth floor, where the emblem of the Ministry of Interior was on display as the elevator doors opened.

"Doris, Mr. Murkomen asked that we visit with him."

"Yes, of course, Dr. Omollo. He asked that you go directly in."

The Honorable Onesimus Kipchumba Murkomen had a spacious office overlooking the city. The three silver domes of the Jamia Mosque were prominent in the city's skyline.

A short elderly man came out from behind a massive desk and, coming over, introduced himself.,

"I am so pleased you had the time to come by. I am Onesimus Murkomen. Please have a seat," he said, indicating a sitting area by one of the large windows. "I get so few visitors who aren't bureaucrats. Your visit is refreshing. I apologize for not being here to meet you when you first arrived. My granddaughter had her first recital that morning, and my wife would have had my ..., well, you understand, if I had missed it."

"We fully understand," I said. "How was the recital? Was it dance or piano?"

"Ballet, and she was a star."

"Prior to your arrival, Sir Charles called and told me about President Ruto's request for assistance. He asked that I keep an eye on you, inferring you had a habit of finding trouble. And then you two disappeared. I was in a quandary. Raymond here has tried to keep me informed. Perhaps you can recount your story one more time," he asked.

An hour later, I concluded my story. His many probing questions stretched a 15-minute tale into an hour. Some heads were going to roll, I was thinking.

"Thank you for your time," he said, signaling that our meeting was over. "Please give Sir Charles my regards. He and I attended Eaton together. He was an upper-class member when I first entered. He took me under his wing, so to speak, and fended off the bullies."

17 Beirut

With my British passport in hand, Harold and I had just landed in
Beirut. Sir Charles had laid the groundwork for us, making a
hotel reservation at the Merry Land Hotel. For a three-star
facility, it was not bad. Located in the hills, thirty minutes from
the city, the Merry Land is a charming boutique hotel.

The hotel was also on the road leading to Amal Choucair's
home in the Lebanese foothills. On the map, a distance of a little
over four miles. On the winding road up the valley, more like
seven.

At ten the next morning, we found a taxi to take us to Mrouj,
the community in which Choucair's home was located. When
asked to take the drive up to the mansion, the driver refused.
Harold offered to double the fare; he reluctantly agreed.
Discharging us at the far side of the circular drive, he took his
fare and made a hasty departure.

Neither Amal nor Amira was expecting us. Three security
guards with automatic rifles descended on us. Demanding to
know why we were there. Unfortunately, it was all in Lebanese.

Sensing the nature of his excitement, I said loudly and slowly, "We are here to see Mr. Choucair."

A young lady came out of the house and, from the veranda, yelled something in Lebanese. We were then herded to the bottom of the steps leading up to the woman.

Taking the lead, "Isabell, we finally meet. I'm George, your cousin."

Clearly taken by surprise, she considers us for a moment and then says in upper-class English, "My name is Amira, there is no Isabell here."

"Is your grandfather home? He is an old friend of my Uncle Alexander."

An old man with a cane joined Amira on the porch. "George, is that you? An old man's eyesight fails me."

Turning and looking directly at Amira, "This is the man from MI5 who helped track down that scum Afram Gurmani, who murdered my granddaughter -- Isabell. And he is right, Alexander Basdakis is an old friend."

"Where are our manners? You two, please come up and have a seat. Refreshments?"

A maid who had quietly appeared quickly scurried off to fetch lemonade and biscuits.

"Now tell me George, what brings you two to Beirut?" asked Amal.

"Would it surprise you if I said we were tracking arms shipments? Shipments to Africa?"

"That sounds exciting," said Amira. "But why are you here?"

"Well, Victor is the captain of one of the boats we intercepted. He is one of your trusted boat captains."

"Not true!" snapped Amira.

Harold looked at Amal and was about to say something when Mr. Choucair cut in, "They've got us Amira. Harold here is with MI6. They've been tracking me for years and know the names of my people, probably even your maid's name. They have even employed my services in the past; perhaps Victor was one."

"So what do you want to know?" he asked, looking back at me.

"We were tasked to help Kenya stem the flow of illegal weapons into their country. I think we've done that by identifying the recipients and the points of inflow. The local authorities can deal with those issues. But I'm, and more so Sir Charles, are left with a question: where are the weapons coming from? I'm hoping you can help us find the answer to that."

18 Answers

We spent the next two days partaking in the Merry Land Hotel's amenities. That is to say, we slept in and hung out at the pool in the afternoon. A brief call to Sir Charles suggested we stay put. The boat on which we were held captive was making its way through the Suez Canal. MI6 analysts were expecting it to head to Beirut.

On the third day, I received a call from Amira, who, with a much friendlier voice, said, "George, Amal asked that I call you to invite you back so we can continue our discussion. I'll have a car pick you up in an hour."

Turning to Harold, "Get dressed, I just received a summons to the big house. Transportation will be here shortly."

When the car arrived, the driver refused to take Harold.

"Look, Waleed," that was the name on his nametag, "you call Mr. Choucair and tell him I'm not coming without Harold."

The poor boy looked terrified, "She'll skin me if I return without you."

"Well, you've got a problem. It's both of us, or neither."

As we got out of the car, Amal greeted us. "I'm happy to see Mr. Lynn could join us."

"Come up into the house," he continued, "there is someone I want you to meet."

Standing in the foyer was Victor Shevchenko. If he was surprised to see us, he kept it well hidden.

"I think you know Victor," said Amira, who was standing nearby.

Without missing a beat, "Victor. I didn't expect to see you here. You left a pissed-off Madam Woo in Zanzibar when you escaped. In her rage, she had one of the men guarding you shot." Not true, but good for Madam Woo's reputation.

"You know him?" exclaimed Amira, surprised that Harold and my story held together.

"Yes, as I told you earlier, he is the one who was going to throw Harold and me overboard. Madam Woo rescued us."

"Victor, what are you doing here? Back for another load of arms? I believe Simon Kigondu has canceled his order; he is dealing with other personal life-threatening problems."

"That is what we understand," said Amira. "We have other customers."

19   The Troubles

The following morning, we were moved from the Merry Land Hotel to Amal's home at his instance. *'I'll not have Alexander's nephew staying at a hotel when I have a place for him,"* he said, *"and my people tell me there is the potential for some unpleasantness in the city.'*

"I'm sorry, Amira isn't here to welcome you," said Amal as we got out of the car he had sent for us. There appears to be growing unrest in the city. She went to the docks to check on our warehouse."

"When did she leave?" I asked. "Harold and I can go and watch her back."

"No need to worry about that girl, " said Amal. "Her security detail scares me."

Later that day, smoke could be seen coming from various quarters of the city. Amal kept trying to get Amira, or anyone in his organization, on his cell phone.

"No one is answering," he said, mostly to himself. "The cell towers must be down."

"Use the landline," Harold suggested.

Amal laughed. "We haven't had a functioning landline in ten years."

"There is no television reception; the stations must be off the air," said the butler. "I've taken the liberty of getting the old radio set out of storage. The international news on Al Jazeera radio is talking about Lebanon."

"Thank you, Bennie," said Amal. "I'm glad to see one of us is still thinking."

Over the next half hour, we learned there were two armed militias fighting for control of Beirut: the *Marada Movement*, a pro-Syrian group, and the *Free Patriotic Movement*, which was aligned with the country's Druze and Christian communities.

Fighting went on all night. It was early in the morning when Al Jazeera announced that it appeared the *Free Patriotic Movement* was in control of Beirut. The Israeli air force, in support of the Patriotic Movement , had taken out the Marada Movement's base camp on the edge of the city.

Al Jazeera spent the early morning hours talking about the destruction in the city's port area. Midmorning, the local TV station was back on the air. The unedited tape showed large stretches of debris in the commercial port area. "This looks worse than the explosions that ripped apart the waterfront five years ago," said Amal.

It was only a bit later that the head of Amira's security detail arrived and reported that Amira was missing.

"What do you mean missing?!!" snapped a worried grandfather.

"Sir, she was in the warehouse about ten last night when it exploded. An RPG fired at a police car hit the warehouse and ignited the munitions Amira had us store there. It went off in a fireball. We've been searching all night for her body in the rubble but have not found it."

"Did she get out?" asked a hopeful Amal.

"I don't see how she could have. We were outside the building guarding it as she ordered. We would have seen her if she had."

Amal, looking totally despondent, shuffled over to the rocker on the porch and sat.

"Amal, Harold, and I are going to look for Amira," I yelled from the driveway in front of the mansion as I ushered Amira's man back into his vehicle and directed him to take us to the warehouse, or more aptly, the site of the former warehouse.

20   The Warehouse

The video we saw earlier on the local TV did not do the damage justice. As we got closer to the waterfront, the magnitude of destruction grew. Along the docks, most structures were damaged to some degree, some still burning. Where one large building once stood was a blackened mass of bent metal framing and ash. "This is Amal's warehouse," the driver said.

The three of us got out of the car and walked around the perimeter; the charred remains were still too hot to walk on. There were no fire trucks in the area; they had been pulled back to the business and residential areas.

Cell service, if somewhat spotty, had been restored. I called Amal to report our findings. "I don't know if there is a body in this mess or not. It's still too hot to poke around."

"I'll make some calls," he said, then cut the connection.

Thirty minutes later, a tug pulled alongside the dock and began spraying the site with saltwater using a makeshift pump. At first, the wreckage was hidden beneath a cloud of steam. In time, that cleared. By late afternoon, we were able to start sifting through the debris. The remaining members of Amira's security detail joined us. The additional people helped. A short while later, one called out, "I think I found a body." Harold and I converged on the man as he pointed under the collapsed section of the roof. Two legs were visible.

Everyone there helped in clearing the area. Removing that roof section required our joint effort to flip it over. As it crashed into its new resting place, the charred remains of a body were visible.

"Get a tarp," I ordered.

We gently rolled the body onto the tarp, wrapped it, and placed it in the back of the waiting van. Three vehicles made their way into the foothills to Amal's manor.

Is that Amira's body?" asked Harold.

"I don't know, it's about the right size, but too burned for me to recognize."

Amel had us place the body in one of the garages, which was converted into a makeshift morgue. "Tripoli's pathologist owes me. He will be here in the morning," said Amal.

The following day, the pathologist's report confirmed the body was that of a female, early to mid-30s, and was most likely Amira. The only way to be certain was a DNA test.

Amal agreed to the test. Samples were taken from both the body and Amal. Amal also insisted that a sample be taken from me, given that I was her cousin. "It will be about two weeks before I have the results," said the pathologist.

21 Retirement

I found Amal in the living room, sitting in the same recliner he was in when I retired last night.

"Have you been here all night?" I asked.

He looked up, "I've decided to shut down my operation. I'm old. I have no children. My brother, my estranged brother, bless his soul, wants nothing to do with my business. He's one of those do-gooders who bends to the fickle whims of the masses."

"I have three loyal captains. Two are good at following orders but would flounder if left to their own devices. Victor is capable but has refused my earlier offers to move him into management."

"Amira was to be my successor. Only you and Harold know she is really Isabell. She was a bit hard for my tastes, but effective."

"Did you know she is the one who devised the plan to use her twin sister, Dina, as her body double? Since their birth, Dina was in a local institute here in Beirut. She had the mind of a three-year-old, you know. I'm not sure, but I think Amira killed Dina and planted the body in that London alley."

"I understand you used to be in the smuggling business; do you want to take over?"

I looked at him in surprise, "And you know that how?"

"Your Uncle Alexander. Give him good brandy, and he talks more than an intelligence officer should. But not to worry, he didn't go into detail – but someday tell me about shipping cars to Brazil," he said with a smile.

About then, Harold came into the room. "You two are up early," he said.

"Amal was just telling me he's shutting up his operation, retiring for good."

"Damn, Sir Charles wanted to find the source of those weapons being shipped to Kenya."

Amal looked at Harold as if to say, '*I have my own problems*,' and then said, "Victor will be filling Amira's contract with the oligarchs in the Ukraine." And then added in a brusque tone, "I believe that is the source of the weapons. Why don't you go with him and catch them red-handed?"

Acknowledging the rebuke, Harold added, "Please forgive my impatience. I am sorry for your loss. We can talk about this later."

Amal continued sitting when Bennie appeared, "Breakfast buffet is ready in the dining room," he said.

Later that morning, I was again alone with Amal. "To answer your earlier question, no, I don't want to take over your operation; Maggi would neuter me. But if he is willing, I'd like to employ Victor. I'm thinking of expanding Basdakis Shipping."

With a wink, Amal said, "I see."

"Legitimate cargoes," I added.

"But your comment about having Harold accompany Victor has me thinking, what about both Harold and me joining him?"

"That's okay with me. Talk to Victor."

22 Planning

I found Victor later that morning in the guest quarters located on the other side of the compound.

Catching him by surprise, "Victor, how would you like to come and work for me at Basdakis Shipping. Strictly legitimate work, no smuggling?"

"No! you try take me from Mr. Choucair. I thought you his friend."

"Victor, I'm glad to see your loyalty to Mr. Choucair. He will be talking with you today or tomorrow about his plans. He will be closing his operation after your trip to Odessa. He has no one to take over, and after Amira's death, he's tired. He mentioned he offered you a management position in the past, but you declined. I told him I'd like you to join Basdakis Shipping. He supports that idea. Talk with him and think it over, we will have time to talk later on our trip to Odessa."

"Our trip?"

"Yes," I answered with a smile. "Harold and I will be joining you."

***

Victor's boat, *The Pomegranate*, was a small coastal freighter known as a coaster. It was a WWII relic, one hundred feet long, with a cargo capacity of seventy-five tons, and a maximum speed of eight knots. Ideal for slipping into and out of shallow, seldom-used harbors, but a floating coffin in high seas. Victor had anchored *The Pomegranate* just off the coast near Kaslik, a small resort just north of Beirut, to avoid the unpleasantness of the big city, so he claimed. It was also a good place to avoid customs.

As we got underway with the rising sun at our back, Harold contacted Sir Charles on his satphone to report in. He was told to expect a return call later that day.

Standing on the bridge, I made the mistake of verbally noting seagulls were moving faster than *The Pomegranate.*

"You run shipping company? What you think cargo boats do? *Speedboat maybe?"* said Victor, the insulted ship's captain.

Late that afternoon, lunchtime in London, Sir Charles is back on the line with Harold. Harold hands me the phone, "George, I need you to stop in Athens on your way to Odessa. Your uncle will have some new information for you that I'd prefer not to discuss on the phone."

I asked Victor if we could stop at Athens. He wasn't excited about the idea, but we could stop for twelve hours; he had a schedule to keep.

Eighteen hours later, we were anchored outside Piraeus, Athens' port city. Alexander had arranged for anchorage rights and had paid the necessary fees.

The three of us took the port water taxi to shore.

"Why you bring me?" complained Victor.

"Because you're part of the team now and it's important that you know the details," I said.

We were unlucky catching the end of the morning rush hour. It took us forty-five minutes to get to the GIS Headquarters in downtown Athens. Once there, we were ushered up to Alexander's office.

Alexander, as effusive as ever, "You must be Victor. George has been telling me you may be joining his company. Over the years, Amal has mentioned his dependence on you."

"Okay, gentlemen, have a seat. This won't take long. Sir Charles and I have been discussing your task: find the source of weapons coming from Ukraine. He has discussed this with selected NATO leadership members, and they wholeheartedly support your mission."

"Now, here's the rub. They want to know the details of your plan. Who you are to meet in Odessa? When you plan to meet?

62

Payment details, etc. Too much detail for my liking," said Alexander.

"I smuggle long time. Still alive," said Victor. "That stupid, I tell nothing!"

"Agreed," said Alexander. "I suggested we only provide an approximate date of your arrival, and you call when you are there. They reluctantly agreed. They gave us the number for their man on the ground. A trusted man. You are to call him when you get there."

Harold and I looked at Victor, and he nodded in reluctant agreement. He told Alexander our arrival date in Odessa would be in seven to ten days; transiting the Bosphorus Strait and dealing with corrupt Turkish officials was always time-consuming. And he had to add some time to avoid possible combatants on the Black Sea.

Once *The Pomegranate* was underway, headed for the Dardanelles, Victor confided to us, "I never trust spies, lie to me. We arrive in Odessa five days; I have man I trust. We call him first."

23 Sergey

Our passage through the Dardanelles and the Bosphorus Strait was uneventful. Transit fees for a coastal freighter, the size of The Pomegranate, were minimal; less than four hundred euros. We were required to take on a local pilot for passage through the Bosphorus Strait. This cost a half day while we waited for the Turkish authorities to provide one.

"You bring luck. Last time waited two days," said Victor.

It was slightly less than 400 miles from Istanbul to Odessa. Keeping the coast in sight on our port side made it a little longer, turning a three-day trip into five days. Victor had great distrust in the Russian Navy's promise not to interfere with shipping.

The Pomegranate slowed as it entered Ukrainian waters to take on a passenger. It was after midnight when the speedboat pulled alongside, and the passenger boarded our ship.

The next morning, "This Sergey," said Victor, introducing him to us over morning coffee. "He my Odessa contact. Tells me shipment is at docks but more police activity. Suggest we go home. Not worth risk."

"Not an option," I said. The Pomegranate was carrying consumer goods, clothes, electronics, etc., as a cover. "We go in, deliver our cargo. And for the time being, ignore the arms shipment while you assess the risk."

"And what I do for new cargo?"

"Ah," I quickly thought. "The Greek Orthodox Church is paying you to take war refugees to Greece. I'll call Alexander and have him create a back story. I think he knows the Archbishop of Athens." Victor was skeptical.

We entered the Sukhyi Estuary, Odessa's port, following Sergey's directions to our assigned docking area. We pulled alongside pier 29b. It was located in the far backside of the port. "You wait," said Sergey. "Boris will contact you tomorrow," he told Victor. "No one gets off The Pomegranate. The *Politsia*, our national police," he said, looking at me, "picking up all strangers."

Harold and I retreated to my cabin to make two calls. The first, using the cell phone provided by Alexander, was to the agent NATO had in Odessa, as we were directed to do. The message was brief: "This is Athens. Arrived this morning. Meeting Boris tomorrow."

My second call, on Harold's satphone, was to Sir Charles. We gave him a complete rundown.

***

Returning to the bridge, we found Victor and Sergey with a half-empty bottle of vodka.

"Have a drink," said Victor as Sergey took a swig from the bottle.

"No need for glasses here," observed Harold.

"Victor, who is Sergey?" I asked.

After a quick swig, he told me their story.

In 1991, as everything was falling apart in the old Soviet Union, government officials were seizing anything of value they could. Sergey and I, both in the Soviet Merchant Marine, decided to take the SS Dookie, the freighter we were assigned to. It was a 3rd rate freighter, a seventy-five-tonner with a crew of seven.

I was the first mate and Sergey the boson's mate. We convinced two other crew members to join and got the Dookie underway late one night. Not having any idea where to go, we headed to the Bosphorus Strait. At that time, Soviet ships had free passage through the strait.

I had heard Beirut was home to several arms dealers: smugglers. At a Beirut waterfront bar, I learned of a Mr. Choucair. It took two days to find the man. Mr. Choucair was impressed to learn we had absconded with a Soviet freighter. He offered to take us under his wing if we worked for him. A deal was struck, and the Dookie became The Pomegranate with the appropriate papers, forged as they may have been, and Greek registration.

Sergey and I had a few years to repay Mr. Choucair for his investment in obtaining papers renaming the Pomegranate . In 2005, I took an advance from Mr. Choucair and bought out Sergey, who wanted to retire to Odessa. That debt was repaid in five years, leaving me as the sole owner of The Pomegranate.

The following morning, Boris arrived in an old delivery van. As a pretext, he brought a package aboard, asking for the captain's signature.

Victor introduced Harold and me, "Boris, these are George and Harold, buyer representatives. They want see goods."

"No. Not part of deal."

"Victor, prepare the ship to leave," I said.

Boris stood, mouth agape, "You can't do that!" He stammered.

"Let me make it simple for you, Boris. You deal with me, or there is no deal."

Flummoxed, he pulled his cell phone out and called his boss, explaining his difficulties. Finally, "Okay, they come."

As the van made a U-turn on the pier, the three of us were down the gangway and slipped into the open side door, and we were off.

24 Odessa Underground

We didn't go far. When the van's sliding door opened, we were in a small warehouse with several unsavory armed men watching us.

"Hello, you must be George," the man said, shaking my hand and turning to Harold, "Harold, I assume. I'm Kyrylo, and this is my little enterprise. I'm told you represent Amira."

"Well, we did, she's dead. There was some political disturbance in Beirut earlier this month; she was a casualty. Mr. Choucair wants to honor her open contracts, of which you are one."

Kyrylo took all this in and gave some direction to one of his men in Ukrainian. Then turned to me, "Let me give you a quick tour of our goods." He pulled back the tarps covering several crates. "As you can see, the latest small arms," pointing to crates with NATO markings and nomenclature for a variety of weapons.

"Can you open that one and the one over there?" said Harold.

"Yes, but first let's talk about money."

About this time, two men, dragging a third, came in. After a brief exchange I didn't understand, Kyrylo turned to us, "He followed the van here, who is he?"

Politsia? said Victor.

No, he Westerner, look at clothes," said Boris.

Kyrylo stood there looking at the man. He pulled out a folding knife, opened it, and started slicing a piece of paper. "I keep it very sharp, he said. Now tell me who you are before I start carving your face."

At first, blood, the man screamed, "Okay, I'll talk. I work for NATO."

"And why are you here?" Kyrylo asked as he rubbed the flat of the blade across the man's forehead.

Looking at us, "To follow them."

"Why?"

"I was told to. We didn't trust them to report back."

Kyrylo snapped his fingers, and guns were aimed at us. "You two are coming with me," said Kyrylo as our hands were zip-tied and hoods placed over our heads.

"Boris, take Victor back to his boat and leave two men with him. He is not to leave."

We were led back to the van, which I assume was the same one that had brought us to the warehouse, and we drove and drove. Most of the day was spent on country roads, but toward the end, the roads felt as if they were in a city or large town, stopping at red lights and horns honking, etc.

When we stopped, the hoods were taken off. It appeared we were in a parking garage. Harold and I were led, some might say pushed, to an elevator in the center of the garage. Kyrylo punched '7,' the seventh floor I assumed. In the lobby, we met a lightly bearded man in a business suit.

"Kyrylo, this is no way to treat our guest. Untie them."

My hands were numb. Cutting the zip tie allowed more blood to flow to my fingers; they began to tingle back to life.

Turning to me, "George, or are you Harold?"

"George and you are?"

"Oh, excuse my manners, I'm Denys Shmyhal, Ukraine's Defense Minister."

"We find ourselves in a rather delicate position here. Our MI6 backdoor has kept us posted on your activities. I've been expecting you."

"What the hell," snapped Harold. Even members of their central government are taking bribes.

"No," said the Defense Minister. "We keep telling NATO, enough with the small arms. We need artillery shells, ground-to-air missiles – high-tech weapons. And they keep sending us surplus small arms."

"We are now selling them on the black market to get cash for clandestine operations. That operation last year that destroyed a number of Russian aircraft deep inside their territory was funded by sales on the black market, as were recent attacks on the Russian fleet in the Black Sea."

"The West doesn't provide enough funding for these operations?" I ask.

"Of course they do. But we must report how we use the money. Can you imagine the response we'd get if I told America, 'We're going to use your money to attack Moscow.' And what do you think the chances are that our plans would be leaked to the western press? No, it's best if we develop a covert funding source."

But to discuss our black market sales of the NATO weapons is not why I brought you here.

25 The Plan

"In 1994, Ukraine signed the Budapest Memorandum on Security Assurances along with Russia, the United States, and several western countries," said Denys Shmyhal. "In that Agreement, we gave up the nuclear weapons we retained from the former Soviet Union. In exchange, the signatories guaranteed Ukraine's security."

"You can see how well that has worked out," scoffed the Defense Minister.

"Some here were cynical of the Memorandum and took steps to retain three nuclear devices. Now, when you report back to Sir Charles, he will be skeptical of our claim. I will provide you with the serial numbers of the main units and supporting equipment and photographs that document our retention of the warheads. Tell Sir Charles to give copies of the documents to the Russians. They can compare serial numbers with their records and see that they have bombs unaccounted for."

"I'm also giving you a thumb drive with a video showing our technicians preparing one of those devices for use. Your video specialist will be able to determine its authenticity."

"We also have a choice of delivery methods: a conventional rocket, by land on a truck delivering produce, or a containership to Kaliningrad or Saint Petersburg.

"That last choice would affect the Baltic States," Harold muttered.

"Yes," said the Minister. And that should give the West a greater incentive to help bring this war to an end.

"Now you are probably asking yourself why I'm telling you all this. We want the West to know that if Russia uses a tactical nuclear weapon, we will respond in kind. More importantly, we want Russia to know."

"And why do you think they will believe us, that this isn't all a smoke screen manufactured by an artificial intelligence program?"

"By itself, perhaps not. But this will corroborate other leaked messages and of our President's threats aimed at Russia," said the Minister.

"Okay, now you two are going back to London. My people will take you to the Polish border. We will alert Sir Charles of your departure from Kiev."

"What happened to the NATO agent Kyrylo was holding?" I asked.

"Oh, he is fine. The cut he received was stitched up, and he is now being held by the *Politsia*, charged as a foreign agent, but will eventually be released, claiming a misunderstanding."

We were driven to the border, where Embassy personnel were waiting for us. Sir Charles had an old Learjet waiting, staffed with an older steward and no bar service. "I guess we are not in Sir Charles's good graces," said Harold. "At least we don't have hoods over our heads this time."

I prepared our preliminary report on a laptop the steward reluctantly provided. Harold read it and made a few additions.

26 Our Path to the Past

We were deposited in an old hotel in the center of London and told we would be picked up the next morning. We had no money and were hungry. We had not eaten since morning, Odessa time. That was fourteen hours ago. Harold called an old mate at the MET, and we were soon seated in the MET's cafeteria.

"The food here is not fancy," said Harold, "but it's good, everyday English food."

Harold's friends wanted a blow-by-blow accounting of Harold's adventures since his temporary transfer to MI6.

"Sorry, mate, if I talked, my friend here would have to kill you. But it has been exciting. The assignment has taken me to some of the world's most luxurious resort areas. Someday I'll have to write a book."

I rolled my eyes and said, "It would be mostly fiction."

The three MET officers we were with spotted us to a few pints before we were returned to the hotel.

Upon seeing the hotel, Annie, one of the officers, said, "Is this the best they could do for you? Our vice squad raided this place last month."

Thankfully, the hotel had a breakfast bar for its guests. I was able to get my coffee, a danish, and some fresh fruit. Sir Charles's car arrived at ten to pick us up.

Things were looking better when we arrived at his office. His secretary offered us coffee and escorted us into the inner office.

"Sir Charles will be with you shortly," said Peggy, his personal secretary.

Twenty minutes later, Sir Charles entered the room.

"My driver said you were staying at a second-rate hotel. I've taken the liberty of moving you to the Carlton Tower, George, I believe you've stayed there before."

The Carlton Tower Hotel was just off Hyde Park. Room rates had to be upward of £ 400 a night.

"I've read your report and shared it with a few others here on the sixth floor. We're impressed. The material provided by Denys Shmyhal is most interesting. The videos are being analyzed by our technicians in the basement as we speak."

"Dr. Ambrose Kent, recently the dean of one of the colleges at Oxford, was a member of NATO's team that oversaw the destruction of Soviet nuclear stockpiles in the Ukraine. Arrangements were being made for a visit."

"In the meantime, I'm glad to report that President Ruto in Nigeria is happy. You two helped solve some of his problems. Onesimus Murkomen, my old classmate, couldn't praise you enough."

"Just for your information, *The Pomegranate* left Odessa this morning with a shipment of arms. Since NATO's man on the ground has been compromised, we are not sure where the ship is headed. Our best guess is Algeria. The weapons are, we think, going to the Polisario Front in Western Sahara."

***

Dr. Ambrose Kent was living in a retirement home in the Cotswolds. He was in his late 90s and confined to a wheelchair. We accompanied Sir Charles to the Sunny Vista Home where Dr. Kent was waiting.

Sir Charles's black limousine, accompanied by his security detail, elicited, "My, this is the most excitement we've had around here," from Dr. Milne, the home's administrator. "Dr. Kent is waiting for you in the atrium."

Entering, we found a wizened old man, wrapped in a shawl, "Sir Charles, I assume. I'd get up to greet you, but my legs won't cooperate."

Dr. Kent's body may have deteriorated, but his mind and sense of humor were sharp.

"Dr. Kent," started Sir Charles, "we have recently received disturbing information regarding Soviet nuclear weapons stored in the Ukraine. I understand you were part of the team that sorted out that issue back in the '90s. That is what we would like to discuss with you, but given the topic's sensitivity, we need a private space." This was said as an aide with a meds cart walked by.

"There is a gazebo in the garden, would that do?" suggested Dr. Milne, who had accompanied us to the atrium.

"Well, it would be better than here," said Sir Charles. "Harold, if you could manage the wheelchair, and Dr. Milne, if you could point us in the right direction, we will make our way out there."

It was a very pleasant day, with temperatures in the mid to high 70s and not a cloud in the sky.

27 Soviet Shell Game

The gazebo was in a patch of flowers, a good fifty yards from the nearest ears. Dr. Kent was quite pleased to be outside. "I only get outside once in a blue moon. If it's not raining, it's too cold. But today is beautiful. Now, what can I do for you? I'm sure you didn't come all this way to hear an old man rumble on about the weather."

"That is true," said Sir Charles. "We've received some disturbing information that ties back to 1994 when you were a member of the UN Team implementing the Budapest Memorandum on Security Assurances for the Ukraine. George, would you take it from here?"

I picked it up from the point of Denys Shmyhal's claims that some nuclear weapons remained in Ukraine after the Budapest Memorandum was signed. I described what MI6 had cleared for me to divulge.

Dr. Kent was clearly troubled by this. "Since the team's last meeting in Kiev in 1995, I've felt the Soviets had lost control of their nuclear weapons stockpile. Let me give you some background."

During the Cuban Missile Crisis, the Soviets dispersed their nuclear weapons stockpile. They moved weapons to Ukraine, Belarus, and some to the Stans. Record keeping was surprisingly rudimentary.

The weapons moved to Ukraine were a mix of old atomic bombs and newer hydrogen bombs. The latter were well accounted for, but the atomic bombs, that's another story.

The atomic bombs were relics from the '50s. Much smaller yields than the hydrogen bombs, but two to three times larger in physical size.

Of the two or three dozen, I forget the exact number, there may have been several missing from those listed in the Soviet inventory. But as I said, their record keeping was rudimentary. It was never clear if the discrepancy was caused by the 'musical chairs' the Soviets were playing with the bombs, or if they were being hidden by the Ukrainians, or if they ever existed.

"That's a troubling story," said Sir Charles.

"I suggest you have your people compare the serial numbers Shmyhal provided with those of the old Soviet atomic bombs that the UN committee had, if those records still exist. If the numbers are sequential, he may be telling you the truth," said Dr. Kent.

"You mentioned they were larger than the hydrogen bombs," said Harold. "The Ukrainians have a new cruise missile they call the 'Flamingo.' It has a range of over eighteen hundred miles. Could that carry one of these bombs?"

"No," chuckled Dr. Kent. "We're talking about a bomb the size of a car, and twice as heavy. They would need a bomber."

We thanked Dr. Kent for his time, and as we headed back to London, Sir Charles called his office, asking his assistant to contact Brussels to see if NATO had any records from the 1994 Budapest Memorandum, and then said to us, "I think they have one."

Looking puzzled, Harold responded, "One what?"

"A bomber, or something close enough that would work," said Sir Charles. "America gave them a half dozen old C-130 cargo planes. President Zelenski claimed the planes were needed to move troops and military supplies around the country. One of these planes could fly deep into Russian territory, carrying all three bombs. All the air crew needs to do is open the back loading ramp while airborne and push a bomb out."

28 Game On

Calls had been made to Brussels by the time we were back in London. NATO's archivists thought there was a copy of the Budapest Memorandum along with all related records stored somewhere in the basement. He would have his staff look. Two days later, he called back to report they had found the records, asking, "What would MI6 like to know?"

"You two know what the story is," said Sir Charles after calling us to his office. "You're going to Brussels to see what is in those records."

Taking an MI6 Learjet, we were in Brussels two hours later, meeting with the archivist, Monsieur Broodthaers.

"I've had the records brought up; they are in the room next door," he said, and indeed they were, all seven boxes.

Harold and I laid our jackets aside, and each of us started with a box.

"What are you looking for? Can I help?" our host asked.

"Thank you, but no. If we find what we hope not to find, you would have to be held incommunicado."

Looking a bit nervous, Monsieur Broodthaers said, "I'll leave you to it," as he left the room.

It was in the last box, why is it always the last box, that we found the list of nuclear devices and their serial numbers. The devices were listed as 'Hydrogen' or 'Atomic'. The three serial numbers we had for the three bombs that Denys Shmyhal claimed the Ukrainians had were sequential to the five atomic bombs listed here.

"Shit, Sir Charles is not going to like this," I muttered more to myself than anyone else.

Leaving Harold, I went back to Broodthaers' office, "Monsieur, is there a copy machine we could use?"

"Yes, just down the hall. Can I help?" he somewhat timidly asked, and I again declined his offer.

We made copies of the pertinent documents and repackaged the boxes as we had found them.

On our way out, I thanked our host and added, "Monsieur Broodthaers, I suggest you secure these boxes in a safe place; they will be needed again."

Back in London, we laid out the copies of the documents we had found for Sir Charles. Harold provided Shmyhal's list of serial numbers for Sir Charles to compare with the Budapest Memorandum's inventory.

"This list supports the Ukraine's claim. Our video techs can find no fault with the video you were given. I think we have to believe Denys Shmyhal's claimes," said Sir Charles. "Peggy," he called out.

"Yes sir," she said, coming into the office. "More coffee?"

"No, please call the Prime Minister's Office and get me on his calendar. Tell them this is urgent."

Sir Charles had an appointment for 4:30 that afternoon. The Evening Star's early edition was on the street at four. The headline:

'UKRAINE HAS NUCLEAR BOMBS'
Confirmed by MI6.

Sir Charles was ushered into 10 Downing Street, where he joined the Minister of Defense in the Prime Minister's private office.

After three hours of heated discussion and numerous calls to allies, a haggard Sir Charles emerged. He had his driver take him to 'his club' where a stiff brandy awaited.

29   Home

After an uneventful flight back to Greece, and a puddle jumper from Athens to Corfu, I was home. I didn't even stop to debrief Alexander; that could wait until later. Maggi and ltl George were waiting.

"No more adventures planned?" asked Maggi. "I had the landline disconnected," she said, "don't want any more calls from your Uncle."

Changing the topic, "How is business at Basdakis Shipping? We might be taking on a new coastal freighter, The Pomegranate."

"Are you still thinking of expanding our operation into the Indian Ocean?"

"And what is wrong with that idea?" I asked. "I have a potential partner in Rajee Gupta in Mumbai. And I found a suitable warehouse in Mombasa and possibly someone to manage local operations there. Sunil Shikanda son. Sunil mentioned his son was working for a local import/export company but was looking for a more challenging position."

Now, if truth be told, Maggi was the person behind the success of the Basdakis Shipping Brokerage Co. When we first met, the company was little more than a front for Uncle Christof's smuggling operation, and I was his man in Greece. He set the company up, but for various reasons, scrutiny by US Customs being one, I was the owner.

Maggi and Christof became good friends, both having a shared interest – my well-being. Maggi insisted I give up smuggling if we were to be a couple. There was a congenial parting of the way between Christof and me. In fact, he later sold me, at very favorable terms, his US coastal shipping company: five small freighters that transported legal freight from middle America to the Gulf and Atlantic coasts. Under the Joans Act of 1920, owners of freighters plying American waterways had to be American citizens. As a dual citizen of Greece and the US, I qualified.

"Tell me about The Pomegranate," she asked.

"It is owned by Victor Shevchenko, who is also its captain. He works for Amal Choucair, the arms dealer, my cousin Isabell's grandfather. Isabell, going by the name Amira, was running his weapons smuggling business. She was killed in the recent hostilities in Beirut. Amal is devastated and is closing his operation."

86

"And you are proposing we take on this Victor, a weapons smuggler," snapped Maggi.

"No, Victor and I agreed he would only handle legal cargo."

"You've already made a deal with him!" shouted Maggi.

This was going downhill fast. "No, we were just talking about a possible future," I said defensively. "I told him I have to talk it over with you."

Somewhat placated, "Let's think it over, over the next few days. You might have a good idea here."

***

Later that week, there was a call from Uncle Alexander on the new landline. He asked that I come to Athens, there was a new development. Maggi rolled her eyes, "Go," she said.

Entering Alexander's office, I was surprised to see Amal Choucair.

Without fanfare, he announced he'd received the DNA analysis from the body found in the burned-out warehouse. "It was not Isabell," he said with surprising fury. I had my men interrogate Amira's guards."

I could only imagine the interrogation methods used.

"It finally came out that she was having an affair with Nicolas Khalaf," he said. "He's the nephew of the *Free Patriotic Movement* founder Waddah Daou. Daou is one of the country's current Members of Parliament, a corrupt bastard."

87

"I want you to find her before she does something dumb –
like getting married. I repeatedly warned her not to get involved
with him."

30 Married

I didn't know how to respond. Buying time, "Let me get back to you in the morning."

"She's your cousin!" said Amal.

True, but not a close one, I was thinking.

After Amal left, leaving his hotel number, Alexander and I talked.

"Do you really want to get involved with politics in the Lavant?" he asked. "Loyalties there change faster than you change your underwear."

"I know. But …"

"Maggi is not going to be happy," he said, stating the obvious.

We both knew what my answer would be.

Later, after telling Maggi I was going to Lebanon again and eliciting the reaction Alexander predicted, she calmed down.

"She's your blood," said Maggi. "You have to find her." If nothing else, the Greeks had an unbending loyalty to family.

The following morning, I called Amal from Alexander's office, "Okay, I'll look for Isabell. What time is your flight? I'll return to Beirut with you."

"George, it struck me late last night that the *Free Patriotic Movement* is as close to Israel as any Lebanese party," said Alexander. "They and the Mossad may be sharing information. You might want to consider contacting the fellow we helped last year, Samuel Horneck, I believe his name was. As I remember, he had some Mossad contacts."

As it turned out, I didn't need help in finding Amira. I simply asked Waddah Daou's secretary where I could find his nephew, Nicolas Khalaf, explaining I was an old school chum of his from Cambridge and would be in Beirut for only a few days."

My smile worked, "Nicolas is on his honeymoon. I think the couple went to Cyprus," she said.

Amel wasn't going to like this. I decided to visit the newlyweds myself to confirm that they were truly married.

I called Alexander to ask him to check the customs visitor records for travelers to Cyprus for the past three months, looking for a Mr. & Mrs. Khalaf.

When I arrived at the Ercan International Airport outside Nicosia, I received a text from Alexander. 'The customs agent reported they arrived two weeks ago and are staying at the St. Raphael Resort.'

I rented a car and, checking the map, found St. Raphael Resort on the south side of the island, about an hour's drive.

After unpacking, I wandered around the resort. Out by the pool, I saw Amira in a lounge chair, a tall drink on the table beside her.

Quietly settling in the chair beside her, "Isabell, or is it Amira?"

Without missing a beat, she responded, "It's Mrs. Nicolas Khalaf. Did my grandfather send you to bring me home?"

"No. He was afraid you'd do something dumb like get married. You know we found a charred body of a woman in the warehouse. He was worried sick it was you. Any idea who it was?"

"No! That's terrible. There was no one in the warehouse when I snuck out the back. She may have been one of Beirut's homeless or hiding from the gunfire. I am so sorry I gave him such a fright."

"So, you and Nicolas eloped. Why? Your grandfather would have given you a spectacular wedding."

"Ha, ha, he has a running feud with Waddah Daou. A year ago, I told Amal I was seeing Nicolas – he nearly choked on his drink; he forbade me from ever seeing him again."

"You know I will be telling him I found you."

"Yes, that will probably be good, give him time to accept the fact I'm married. And if the Gods are good, probably pregnant."

From behind me, a deep voice said, "Amira, you're not trolling for my replacement already, are you?"

Turning, there was a young man, a big young man, holding two icy drinks.

"George, this is Nicolas. Nicolas, George, a distant cousin. My grandfather sent him to rescue me from men like you," she said with a laugh.

I got up and shook his hand. "I understand congratulations are in order, first for a beautiful wife and second for the child she's carrying."

Shocked, he turned to Amira, "You told him?"

"Yes, I can think of nothing else that will get my grandfather's support."

She was right. Later, when I reported back to Amal, he was furious to hear that Amira had married without his consent. But when I mentioned he would soon be a great-grandfather, I could see he would be putty in her hands.

31 Revolt

Major General Sergei Alekseyevich Kniazkov had a dilemma. Earlier in the day, he had received orders from Moscow that he knew he could not execute. General Kniazkov was the commanding officer of Russia's Smolensk Region Bases. Three loosely connected military bases, halfway between Moscow and Belarus.

The order was to arm three Iskander short-range ballistic missiles with tactical nukes. One with the smallest warhead having a five-kiloton yield. The other two with the larger 50-kiloton warheads. The three missiles were to be loaded onto mobile transporter erector launchers.

In five days, the missile with the smallest yield was to be launched, targeting the western edge of the Donbas area, where Russian forces had been bogged down for the past year. The tactical strike was to be carried out at exactly one a.m. Sunday morning, giving the ground commanders time to withdraw their men.

The two missiles having the larger yields were to be held in reserve in the event Ukraine hit back with one of their newly found atomic devices.

The General had directed his aide to have Colonel Leonid Vasilyevich Yakovlev report to him immediately. Colonel Yakovlev was in charge of the tactical missiles.

Within a half hour, the Colonel was standing in front of the General's desk.

"Leonid, I've received orders that I can't comply with," said General Kniazkov. "They involve you." He then went on to read the orders.

Colonel Yakovlev stood in a state of disbelief. No longer at attention. "That will be devastating for Russia," he said. Those old atomic weapons have far more fallout than our tactical weapons.

The General went on, "That egomaniac in the Kremlin is killing our next generation; we've lost more than a million young men in his senseless war. If I comply with this order, I will be an accomplice to bringing hell on earth to Mother Russia."

"I agree," said Colonel Yakovlev, "and I think your staff does also. Before you make any decisions, I suggest you talk with them."

An hour later, a staff meeting was hastily convened. Major-General Sergei Alekseyevich Kniazkov presented his staff with the orders, his proposed response, and asked for their recommendation.

To a man, that is, if one did not count the 'Political Officer', a holdover from the Soviet days, agreed with the General.

The Smolensk Region Bases were put on lockdown. Soldiers were given a synopsis of the situation by the General via the public address system. He concluded with "Gentlemen, fellow soldiers, Russians, what I'm embarking on is a revolt against corrupt politicians that have taken over the Kremlin. In order to save our homeland, I am rejecting these orders. If you are with me, take up your arms and be prepared to fight. If you oppose this action, you have one hour to leave the base."

The Political Officer and thirty-two others walked out the front gate fifty-five minutes later, leaving over three thousand supporting their General.

At five p.m. that day, General Sergei Alekseyevich Kniazkov called Moscow and formally declined the orders.

***

The following morning, the leading elements of the 150th Guards Motor Rifle Division were closing in on the Smolensk Region Bases, prepared to take them by force if Major General Vitaly Terekhin, commander of the division, couldn't bring General Kniazkov to his senses.

The two generals met in a hastily erected tent outside the main gate. A dozen or so others were present, including Colonel Yakovlev. After a heated discussion, General Terekhin concluded, "Sergei, we've been friends a long time, and you are my brother-in-law, but you are forcing me to place you under arrest."

With that, General Terekhin told his aide to arrest the traitors. There was much shuffling of feet behind him as Terekhin's men digested all they had just heard.

Finally, General Terekhin's aide stepped forward and demanded that the General surrender his sidearm and then stated, "General Kniazkov, we are with you."

"Colonel Yakovlev, please escort General Terekhin to our stockade. Make sure he is comfortable," snapped Kniazkov.

As the meeting broke up, one of the attendees was on his cell calling his sister. His sister was the moderator of an illegal podcast on Russia's dark net. It was immediately posted, '*Military units in revolt over Kremlin orders to nuke the Ukraine.*'

The revolt rapidly spread. Senior leaders, civilians, and military were placed under house arrest by sympathetic military units.

The Dunna initiated action to strip the nation's leaders of all authority and issued arrest warrants for several. The Dunna also ordered an immediate ceasefire in the Ukraine and established a team to negotiate peace terms.

32 Снукер

In Kiev, Denys Shmyhal was digesting the news that Russia was standing down. Earlier that day, Moscow had issued orders for a general ceasefire and to disengage from the Ukrainian forces.

His phone had been ringing continuously for the past half hour. He was ignoring it when his secretary stepped into his office. "The President has been trying to get you on the phone. He claims no one is answering. He would like you to come over to his office, if you could break away from ignoring his calls."

The presidential office was in a state of turmoil. Military officers waiting for orders, politicians wanting to know what was happening. And western reporters, trying to interview anyone who would talk to them.

"Denys, quit a zoo out there," said the president. "Reminds me of when I was on the stage with a new routine."

"That Operation *Снукер* of yours worked like a charm. The West bought it and then sold it to Moscow."

Going on, he said, "We really need to keep the details secret until the revolt in Moscow has run its course and we have a peace deal."

"Can you keep that German movie production company quiet for another month or so? It will be worth another twenty percent to them. Tell them the video of the weapons specialist working on the bomb mockups was fantastic. I would have believed it was real if I didn't know it was made in Berlin," said the smiling President.

As they were talking, Sir Charles was having his second cup of morning tea, reading the day's dispatches. He was as surprised as the rest of the West at the rapid collapse of Russia. Reading the latest bit of Ukrainian news, he came across a mention of Operation Снукер. Not recognizing the term, he called in his aide, who was fluent in Russian.

"Brian, what is this term снукер? I don't think I've heard it before.

"Sir, снукер is Russian for snookered.

33 Epilogue

A year later, Maggi and I are on our way to Mombasa to open our African venture. After some thought, Maggi not only agreed to expanding the Basdakis Shipping Brokerage Co., she insisted on it. I can still recall her words.

"After your last boondoggle to Africa, you mentioned finding a place in, I think it was Mombasa, that would be an ideal place for our African expansion. I want to go and see it."

Kenya Airways had a direct flight between Ciro and Mombasa. Sunil Shikanda was there to greet us. He had agreed to be our shipping agent. His son, Ricky, would be the day-to-day manager of the Kenya branch of Basdakis Shipping and Brokerage, to be known as K-BS&B.

Ricky, who was brought up in Lanchester by his grandparents, was a product of English public schools. His education was capped with a stint at a small university, earning himself a degree in business management. As a young man, he moved back to Nairobi to be closer to his parents. He met a girl in the Indian expat community, got married, and now, two children later, needed a secure position that could support him and his family. K-BS&B was a timely venture for both parties.

Sunil had booked us a suite at The Tamarind Village Resort, probably the most expensive lodgings in Mombasa. "Not to worry," he said, "it's off-season and my cousin is the manager. For you, only half price."

'Only half price' was twice what other hotels were charging, but Maggi liked it and I wasn't going to make a fuss. She was anxious to see our new facilities, so we quickly freshened up and met Sunil in the lobby.

As we drove to the commercial docks, Sunil was saying, "As a way of thanking you, Murkomen pulled some strings to help secure your lease on this property – and with an option to buy."

At the far end of the docks, there was an abandoned British naval storage area. "This space has not been used for decades," he was saying. "I had it cleaned up and here it is," he was saying as we drove up to a dilapidated compound overgrown with vines.

Maggi got out of the SUV and started her inspection tour. A half hour later, her assessment was, "This will work. The warehouse appears to be in reasonable shape, but some major work is needed. The office space is probably more than we need; we can grow into it. And I can't believe it has its own private docking facilities. Sunil, you did good. I think we are going to have a good relationship."

"Our first customers are arriving in the next week or so," said Ricky.

Tuning to Maggi, "Rajee Gupta in Mumbai agreed to partner with us. He will be using K-BS&B as his principal shipping hub in Africa. His freighter *The Rajee* is scheduled to be our first customer."

"And we have one other long-term customer, Amira Khalaf." I said. "She resumed management of her grandfather's enterprise, but only legal cargoes -- so she says. I believe *The Pomegranate* is one of the freighters Ricky is expecting."

***

As we waited for our connecting flight at Ciro on our way home, Maggi was saying, "This was a novel idea. I was hoping to expand our business. This will give us a leg up on other Greek companies."

"Oh, I meant to mention it earlier, before we left, Ricky said he received a query from Sino Exports LLC. They have a small shipment going to the Arusha Safari Lodge in Tanzania, supplies for the upcoming tourist season. They are shipping through Mombasa, rather than Dar es Salaam. Arusha is just over the border; it is much easier to get to from the north. I told Ricky to accept the consignment."

"Oh, the lady at Sino Exports identified herself as Madam Woo. She claimed to know you."

Конец
(End)

www.ingramcontent.com/pod-product-compliance
Lightning Source LLC
Chambersburg PA
CBHW021122130626
46554CB00002B/818